GEORGES
SIMENON

DEATH OF A NOBODY
AND
THE MAN IN THE STREET

PENGUIN BOOKS

PENGUIN BOOKS

Published by the Penguin Group. Penguin Books Ltd, 27 Wrights Lane,
London w8 5TZ, England. Penguin Books USA Inc., 375 Hudson Street,
New York, New York 10014, USA. Penguin Books Australia Ltd, Ringwood,
Victoria, Australia. Penguin Books Canada Ltd, 10 Alcorn Avenue, Toronto,
Ontario, Canada M4V 3B2. Penguin Books (NZ) Ltd, 182–190 Wairau Road,
Auckland 10, New Zealand · Penguin Books Ltd, Registered Offices: Har-
mondsworth, Middlesex, England · **These stories have been taken from** *Mai-*
***gret's Christmas* by Georges Simenon, translated by Jean Stewart and**
published by Penguin Books in 1981. This edition published 1995 · Copyright
1947, 1950 by Georges Simenon. Translation copyright © Georges Simenon, 1976.
All rights reserved · Typeset by Datix International Limited, Bungay, Suffolk.
Printed in England by Clays Ltd, St Ives plc · Except in the United States of
America, this book is sold subject to the condition that it shall not, by way of trade
or otherwise, be lent, re-sold, hired out, or otherwise circulated without the
publisher's prior consent in any form of binding or cover other than that in which
it is published and without a similar condition including this condition being
imposed on the subsequent purchaser · 10 9 8 7 6 5 4 3 2 1

CONTENTS

Death of a Nobody

I MURDER OF A MAN IN HIS SHIRT

'Nobodies don't get murdered . . .'

A dozen times, a score of times in the space of two hours this stupid phrase recurred to Maigret's mind, like the refrain of a song heard somewhere or other that haunts one for no reason. It was becoming an obsession, and he found himself muttering the words below his breath; occasionally he varied them:

'Men don't get murdered in their shirts . . .'

It was hot by nine o'clock that August morning. Paris was on holiday. Police Headquarters was almost empty, all its windows wide open over the river, and Maigret had already taken off his jacket when he got the telephone call from Judge Coméliau.

'You ought to go round to the Rue des Dames. There was a crime there last night. The local Superintendent told me a long and complicated story. He's there still, on the spot. The DPP can't get there before eleven o'clock.'

That's how things are always sprung upon one. You're expecting to spend a peaceful day in the shade, and then, before you know where you are . . .

'Coming, Lucas?'

As usual, the Crime Squad's little car was not available and the two men had taken the métro, which smelt of disinfectant and where Maigret had to put out his pipe.

The lower end of the Rue des Dames, near the Rue des Batignolles, was swarming with people in the sunshine; vegetables, fruit and fish were piled high on the little barrows ranged alongside the pavement, which were being assailed by a compact mass of housewives, while the inevitable horde of youngsters seized the opportunity to indulge in their rowdiest games.

A commonplace house, six floors of homes for people of very moderate means, with a laundry and a coal-merchant's shop on the ground floor. A cop on duty by the door.

'The Superintendent's waiting for you upstairs, Monsieur Maigret . . . It's on the third floor . . . Come on, move along, folks . . . There's nothing to see . . . Clear the way, please.'

As usual, the concierge's lodge was full of gossiping women. Doors opened silently on each landing, inquiring faces peeped out. What kind of crime could have been committed in a house like this, inhabited by nobodies, who are usually decent people? A drama of love and jealousy? Even for that the setting was not right.

A door was wide open on to a kitchen, on the third floor. Three or four teenage children were making a noise, and a woman's voice called out from another room:

'Gérard, if you don't leave your sister alone . . .'

It was the shrill, weary voice of one of those women who spend their lives struggling against petty worries. She was the wife of the victim. A door opened, and Maigret was confronted with her and with the local Superintendent; the two men shook hands.

The woman looked at him and sighed, as if to say:

'Another of them!'

'This is Superintendent Maigret,' the local police officer explained. 'He's to be in charge of the investigation.'

'So I shall have to tell him everything all over again?'

It was a living-room with a sewing-machine in one corner and a radio set in another. The open window let in the noise from the street. The kitchen door was open too, letting in the children's chatter, but the woman went to close it and the voices fell silent, as when one switches off the radio.

'It's the sort of thing that only happens to me . . .' she sighed. 'Sit down, gentlemen.'

'Tell me as simply as possible what happened.'

'How can I, when I didn't see anything? It's almost as if nothing had happened . . . He came back at half-past six as usual . . . He'd always been punctual . . . I even had to hustle the children, because he liked to eat as soon as he got back . . .'

She was speaking of her husband, an enlarged photograph of whom hung on the wall facing one of herself. And her air of desolation was not due to the tragedy. Even on the portrait she wore a weary resigned look, as though she bore all the weight of the world on her shoulders.

As for the man, moustached and stiff-collared in his photograph, he was the very image of serenity; he was so neutral, so ordinary that one could have met him a hundred times without noticing him.

'He got back at half-past six, he took off his jacket and hung it up in the wardrobe, for I have to admit that he's always been careful of his things . . . We had dinner . . . I sent the two youngest to play outside . . . Francine, who goes out to work, came back at eight o'clock, and I'd left her dinner on a corner of the table . . .'

She must have told the whole story to the local policeman, but it was obvious that she would repeat it in the same woeful voice as many times as she was asked to, with the anxious glance of someone who's afraid of forgetting something.

She might have been about forty-five, and had probably once been pretty; but she'd been battling for so many years with domestic difficulties!

'Maurice sat down in his corner by the window . . . Look, you're actually sitting in his armchair . . . He read a book, getting up from time to time to switch on the radio . . .'

While at the same time, in all the houses along the Rue des Dames, some hundred other men who, like him, had been working all day in shops or offices, were now relaxing beside open windows, reading an evening paper or a book.

'He never used to go out, you see. Never by himself. Once a week we all went to the pictures together, on Sunday . . .'

From time to time she lost the thread of her talk, because she was listening to the muffled sounds from the kitchen, worrying, wondering whether the children were fighting or something was burning on the stove.

'What was I saying? Oh, yes . . . Francine, who's seventeen, went out again and came home about half past ten . . . The others were in bed already . . . I was preparing the soup for today, ahead of time because I had to go to the dressmaker's this morning . . . Oh Lord! and I didn't even let her know I couldn't come. She must be expecting me.'

One more disaster to worry about!

'We went to bed . . . That's to say we went into the bedroom and I got into bed . . . Maurice always took longer to undress . . . The window was open . . . We hadn't pulled the blinds on account of the heat . . . There was nobody opposite to look in at us . . . it's a hotel . . . People go in and go to bed straight away . . . They seldom hang around by the window . . .'

Maigret was so calm and impassive that Lucas wondered if his Chief was falling asleep. But from time to time a puff of smoke could be seen escaping from the lips that gripped the stem of his pipe.

'What else can I tell you? It *would* happen to me . . . He was talking ... I've forgotten what he was talking about, but he'd just taken off his trousers and he was folding them. He was in his shirt ... He was sitting on the edge of the bed ... He'd taken off his socks and he was rubbing his feet because they were sore ... I heard a noise outside ... Like ... like a car backfiring, or hardly as loud ... It went *pshuittt* ... Yes, *pshuitt*! ... A bit like when the air gets into a tap. I wondered why Maurice had stopped talking in the middle of a sentence. I must admit that I was beginning to drop off, because I'd had a tiring day ... There was a silence, and then he said softly, in a funny sort of voice: "Oh, hell!"

'That surprised me, because he didn't often swear. He wasn't that sort. I asked him: "What's the matter?"

'And then I opened my eyes, because they'd been shut until then, and I saw him topple forward.

'"Maurice!" I cried.

'A man who's never fainted in his life, d'you understand? ... He wasn't very tough maybe, but he was never ill ...

'I got up ... I kept on speaking to him ... He was lying face downwards on the mat ... I tried to lift him up, and I saw blood on his shirt.

'I called Francine, our eldest. And do you know what Francine said to me, when she looked at her father?

'"What have you done, maman?"

'Then she went downstairs to telephone ... She had to wake up the coal-merchant ...'

'Where is Francine?' Maigret asked.

'In her room ... She's getting dressed ... Because we'd never even thought about dressing, all night long ... Just look at me ... The doctor came, then the police, then Monsieur ...'

'Will you leave us?'

5

She did not understand at first, but repeated:

'Leave what?'

Then she disappeared into the kitchen, where she could be heard scolding the children in a monotonous voice.

'Another quarter of an hour of that would have driven me round the bend,' sighed Maigret, drawing a deep breath by the window.

One could not have said exactly why. She may have been a very decent woman, but she exuded a depressing atmosphere which made the very sunlight coming in through the window seem dim and almost gloomy. Everything around her became so dreary, so futile and monotonous that one began to wonder if the street was really there, practically within one's reach, teeming with life and light, with colours, sounds and smells.

'Poor beggar . . .'

Not because he was dead, but because he had lived!

'By the way, what was his name?'

'Tremblet . . . Maurice Tremblet . . . Forty-eight years old! . . . According to his wife, he was cashier with a firm in the Sentier district . . . Let's see, I put down the address: Couvreur et Bellechasse, dealers in *passementerie*.'

Passementerie – gold lace and braid – into the bargain!

'You know,' the police officer explained, 'I thought at first that it was she who had killed him . . . I had just been woken from my first sleep . . . In the chaos that reigned here, with the children all talking at once and her shouting at them to keep quiet, and then telling me the same story over and over again – more or less what you've just heard – I thought at first that she must be crazy or half crazy . . . Particularly as my constable had just been putting her through it:

'"I don't want to hear about all that," he was saying to her. "I want to know why you killed him! . . ."'

'And she was saying: "Why should I have killed him and what could I have killed him with?"'

'There were some neighbours in the stairway ... It was the local doctor, who's going to send me his report, who declared that the bullet had been fired from a distance, probably from one of the windows across the street ... So I sent my men over to the *Hôtel Excelsior*.'

The same little phrase kept recurring to Maigret's mind:

'Nobodies don't get murdered ...'

Particularly a nobody in his shirt-sleeves, sitting on the edge of the double bed, rubbing the soles of his feet.

'Did you discover anything over there?'

Maigret scrutinized the windows of the hotel, which was more of a lodging house. A plaque of imitation black marble read: 'Rooms by the month, week or day. Running water, H and C.'

It was pretty shabby too. But like the house, like the Tremblets' flat, its shabbiness was hardly in keeping with such dramatic events. It was decent shabbiness, respectable mediocrity.

'I began with the third floor, where my men found the lodgers in bed. There was plenty of grumbling, as you can well imagine. The proprietor was furious and threatened to lodge a complaint. Then it occurred to me to go up to the fourth floor. And there I found an empty room, just opposite the right window, if you see what I mean; a room that was supposed to be occupied; it had been taken a week ago by a certain Jules Dartoin. I questioned the night porter. He remembered having pulled the cord to let somebody out shortly before midnight, but he didn't know who it was ...'

Maigret finally brought himself to open the door of the bedroom, where the body of the victim was still lying partly on the rug, partly on the floor, at the foot of the bed.

'Apparently he was shot through the heart, and death was practically instantaneous ... I thought I'd better wait for the police surgeon to come and extract the bullet ... He's expected at any time now, with the people from the DPP.'

'About eleven o'clock ...' Maigret said absentmindedly.

It was now a quarter past ten. Down in the street the housewives were still doing their shopping around the barrows, and a pleasant smell of fruit and vegetables drifted up in the warm air.

'Nobodies don't ...'

'Have you searched the man's pockets?'

This had obviously been done, for his clothes were lying in a heap on the table, whereas according to his wife Tremblet had folded them neatly before going to bed.

'Everything's here ... A purse ... Cigarettes ... A lighter ... Keys ... A wallet containing a hundred francs and photographs of his children.'

'The neighbours?'

'My men have questioned everybody in the house ... The Tremblets have lived here for twenty years ... They took two extra rooms when the family increased ... There seems to be nothing to say about them ... Regular habits ... nothing out of the way ... A fortnight's holiday every year in the Cantal, where Tremblet comes from originally ... They had no visitors except, occasionally, a sister of Madame Tremblet's; her maiden name was Lapointe and she came from Cantal too. Her husband always left at a regular time to go to his office, taking the métro at Villiers station ... He came back at half-past twelve, left again an hour later and returned home at half-past six ...'

'It's idiotic ...'

Maigret spoke almost unconsciously. Because it really was 8 idiotic. Because such a crime was inconceivable.

There are a hundred reasons for killing people, but such reasons are, as it were, catalogued. After thirty years in the police force one immediately knows what sort of crime one is dealing with.

An old woman, a shopkeeper, may be killed for the sake of the money in her till or the savings hidden in her mattress. Murders are committed out of jealousy, or because of . . .

'He wasn't mixed up in politics?'

Maigret went into the next room to look at the book the man had been reading the night before. It was a cloak-and-dagger story in a gaudy cover.

Nothing had been stolen. There had been no attempt at theft. And it was not a random crime. On the contrary, it must have been carefully prepared, since it had meant taking a room in the hotel opposite and procuring a rifle – probably an air-gun.

This could not have been done by just anybody. And it could not have been done to just anybody. Whereas Tremblet's name might well have been Mr Just-Anybody!

'Aren't you going to wait for the men from the DPP?'

'I'll probably be back here before they leave. Be kind enough to stay and put them in the picture.'

In the next room a row was going on; presumably Madame Tremblet, née Lapointe, was having an argument with her children.

'How many has she, by the way?'

'Five . . . Three boys and two girls . . . One of the sons, who had pleurisy last winter, is staying with his grandparents in the country . . . He's thirteen and a half.'

'Coming, Lucas?'

Maigret was not anxious to see Madame Tremblet again just yet, nor to hear her moaning, 'It's just my luck . . .'

9

He went downstairs, treading heavily; once again, doors opened as he passed, and people were whispering behind them. He nearly went into the coal-merchant's shop to have a glass of wine, but it was full of an inquisitive crowd waiting for the arrival of the men from the DPP, and he chose rather to make for the Rue des Batignolles, where nothing was known about the sensational affair.

'What'll you drink?'

'Same as you, Chief.'

Maigret mopped his brow, with a mechanical glance at his reflection in the mirror.

'What do you think about it?'

'That if I'd had a wife like that . . .' Lucas fell silent.

'You go and inquire about the fellow in the *Hôtel Excelsior* . . . You probably won't find out much, because a man who goes about things the way he did . . . Hey, taxi!'

It would go down on the expense account! It was too hot to stifle in the métro or wait for a bus at the street corner.

'I'll see you again at the Rue des Dames . . . Otherwise this afternoon, at the Quai.'

Nobodies don't get themselves killed, for heaven's sake! Or if they do, it's on a large scale, in a war or a revolution. And if it should happen that nobodies kill themselves, they can hardly do it with an air-gun while they're busy rubbing their feet.

If only Tremblet had had a foreign-sounding name, instead of just being a native of Cantal! Then one might have believed that he belonged to some secret society of his compatriots.

He didn't look the sort of person to get murdered, definitely! And that was just what was so disturbing. The apartment, the wife, the kids, the husband in his shirt-sleeves, and the bullet that went *pshuitt* . . .

10

Maigret, sitting in his open taxi, puffed at his pipe and shrugged his shoulders. For a moment he thought of Madame Maigret, who would undoubtedly say with a sigh:

'Poor woman!'

Because women are always sorry for the woman when a man dies.

'No, I don't know the number. Rue du Sentier, yes . . . Couvreur et Bellechasse . . . It must be a big firm . . . founded eighteen hundred and something . . .'

He was furious. He was furious because he could not understand and he hated not understanding. The Rue du Sentier was crowded. The driver stopped to make inquiries and just as he was hailing a passer-by Maigret read the words *Couvreur et Bellechasse*, in elegant gilt script, on a house-front.

'Wait for me . . . I shan't be long.'

He couldn't be sure of that, but the heat made him lazy. Particularly when most of his colleagues and inspectors were on holiday. Particularly when he had promised himself a nice relaxed day in the office.

First floor on the right. A suite of gloomy rooms that looked like vestries.

'Monsieur Couvreur, please.'

'On private business?'

'Extremely private.'

'I'm sorry, Monsieur Couvreur died five years ago.'

'And Monsieur Bellechasse?'

'Monsieur Bellechasse is in Normandy. If you would like to speak to Monsieur Mauvre . . .'

'Who is he?'

'The manager . . . He's at the bank at the moment, but he'll be back shortly.'

'Is Monsieur Tremblet in?' A shot in the dark.

'I beg your pardon, who did you say?'

'Monsieur Tremblet . . . Maurice Tremblet . . .'

'I don't know him . . .'

'Your cashier . . .'

'Our cashier is called Magine, Gaston Magine . . .'

Maigret, whose mind must have run in stock phrases that day, said to himself that you could have knocked him down with a feather.

'Will you wait for Monsieur Mauvre?'

'Yes, I'll wait for him.'

He waited amid a sickly smell of cardboard and *passementerie*. Fortunately not for too long. Monsieur Mauvre was a man of sixty, clad in decent black from head to foot.

'You wanted to speak to me?'

'Superintendent Maigret of the Police Judiciaire.'

If he had hoped to impress Monsieur Mauvre, he had miscalculated.

'And to what do I owe the honour? . . .'

'You have on your staff a cashier named Tremblet, I believe?'

'We had one . . . A long time ago . . . Wait a minute . . . It was the year our Cambrai branch was modernized . . . Seven years ago . . . Yes . . . Not quite seven, for he left us in the middle of the spring.'

And, adjusting his pince-nez:

'It is seven years since Monsieur Tremblet was on our staff.'

'Have you never seen him since?'

'Not personally.'

'Had you any complaint to make of him?'

'None at all. I knew him quite well, for he joined the firm only a few years after I did . . . He was a conscientious, reliable employee. He gave in his notice in a perfectly regular way, for family reasons, I believe ... Yes, he told us he was going to settle in his native province, Auvergne or Cantal, I cannot remember exactly ...'

'You never discovered any irregularities in the accounts he kept?'

Monsieur Mauvre shuddered, as though at a personal indictment.

'No, Monsieur. *Such things do not occur in our firm.*'

'Was there anything to suggest that Monsieur Tremblet had any affairs, or any bad habits?'

'No, Monsieur. Never. And I am sure there was nothing of the sort.'

Curtly. And if Maigret did not understand that he was going too far, in spite of being a Police Superintendent ...

He went on, nonetheless:

'It's odd, because, for the past seven years, until yesterday, Monsieur Tremblet left home every day to come to this office and, every month, handed over his pay packet to his wife ...'

'I am sorry, but that's quite impossible!'

Maigret was being given the hint to remove himself.

'In short, he was an exemplary employee?'

'An excellent employee.'

'And nothing in his behaviour ...'

'No, Monsieur, nothing. You'll excuse me, but two important customers from the provinces are expecting me ...'

Phew! It was almost as stifling as the flat in the Rue des Dames. Maigret was glad to get back to the street and to the taxi, whose driver had had time for a glass of white wine and Vichy at the nearest bistro and was now wiping his moustache.

'Where do we go now, Monsieur Maigret?'

For all the taxi drivers knew him, and that was rather nice too.

'Rue des Dames, old man . . .'

And so, for the past seven years, Maurice Tremblet had left home at a specified time to go to his office, and for seven years he'd . . .

'Will you stop somewhere on the way for me to have a quick drink?'

Before facing Madame Tremblet and all the DPP men, who must be getting in one another's way in the flat in the Rue des Dames!

'Nobodies don't . . .'

But was he really such a nobody as all that?

2   THE GINGER-HAIRED MURDERER AND THE CANARY-FANCIER

'What's the matter with you, Maigret? Can't you sleep?'

It must have been half-past two in the morning, and although both windows were wide open on to the Boulevard Richard-Lenoir, Maigret was bathed in sweat and kept tossing about in bed. He had almost dropped off to sleep. But no sooner did he hear his wife's breathing become regular, as she lay beside him, than he started thinking, involuntarily, and of course that meant thinking about the man he called his nobody.

His thoughts were vague and blurred and somewhat nightmarish. He kept going back to the beginning. Rue des Dames, half-past eight in the morning. Maurice Tremblet, finishing dressing in the flat where the mournful Madame Tremblet – he now knew that she was most unsuitably called Juliette – where

Juliette, with her hair in curlers and a look of misery in her eyes, was trying to keep the children quiet in a way that only provoked storms.

'He had a horror of noise, Superintendent.'

Why was it this detail, more than anything else he had been told, that had most impressed Maigret and that kept recurring to his drowsy mind? To have a horror of noise and yet to live in the Rue des Dames, a narrow street crowded with shoppers, surrounded by five squabbling children and a wife who was incapable of keeping them quiet . . .

'He gets dressed, okay . . . He shaves every other day (according to Juliette's evidence). He drinks his *café au lait* and eats a couple of croissants . . . He goes down and makes his way to the Boulevard des Batignolles, to take the métro at Villiers station.'

Maigret had spent most of the afternoon in his office, dealing with unsettled business. During this time the evening papers, at the request of the police, published various photographs of Maurice Tremblet on their front pages.

As for Sergeant Lucas, he went along to the *Hôtel Excelsior* with a pile of photographs: those of all the ex-convicts and shady characters whose appearance corresponded more or less to the description of the murderer, known as Jules Dartoin.

The proprietor of the hotel, an Auvergnat, studied them all, shaking his head.

'Not that I saw a great deal of him, but he wasn't *that kind of man*.'

Lucas, listening patiently, realized what he meant: the lodger with the rifle was not a tough guy; he did not look like a suspicious character.

'You know, when he first came to rent the room by the week, I'd have thought he might be a night watchman . . .

'A dim sort of fellow, middle-aged. We didn't see much of

him, particularly as he only went to his room to sleep and left very early in the morning.'

'Had he any luggage?'

'A little bag such as football players carry their gear in.'

And a moustache. The proprietor said it was red. The night porter said it was grey. It's true that they saw him by different lights.

'He looked shabby. Not dirty, but shabby. I made him pay a week in advance. He took some notes out of a very old wallet in which there weren't many of them . . .'

The chambermaid's evidence. 'I never happened to meet him, for I only did his room in the middle of the morning, after No. 42 and No. 43, but I know one thing: you could tell he was a bachelor.'

Lucas had gone over the room with meticulous care, inch by inch. On the pillow he had found three hairs, one from a moustache. On the enamel wash-stand a scrap of cologne-scented soap, and on the mantelpiece an old comb with several teeth missing.

That was all: not much of a harvest. And yet the laboratory experts had drawn certain conclusions: after working on the hair and the comb for several hours, they declared that the man was aged between forty-six and forty-eight, with red hair turning grey, beginning to grow bald, with a troubled lymphatic system and an unhealthy liver.

But that was not what Maigret was thinking about in his bed. He was thinking of the murdered man.

'He gets dressed, eats, puts on his hat and goes out . . . He walks to the métro in the Boulevard des Batignolles . . .'

Certainly not to go to the office in the Rue du Sentier, to Messrs Couvreur and Bellechasse, where he had not set foot in seven years, but to go heaven knows where.

It occurred to Maigret that in the days when Tremblet was still cashier in the Rue du Sentier the métro was very convenient for him. The Porte de Champerret–Porte des Lilas line is a direct one. Tremblet merely had to get off at Sentier.

And then he remembered that Francine, the daughter, whom he had scarcely seen, had been working for the past year in a Prisunic in the Rue Réaumur. The Rue Réaumur is next to the Rue du Sentier, on the same métro line.

'Can't you sleep?' Madame Maigret asked.

And he said:

'Perhaps you can tell me something. I suppose all the Prisunic shops belong to the same company and follow the same rules. You've been to the République one . . .'

'What are you getting at?'

'Do you know what time those shops open?'

'Nine o'clock.'

'You're sure?' And this seemed to make him so happy that he hummed a little song before falling asleep at last.

'Her mother said nothing?'

Maigret was in his office, at a quarter past nine, and Lucas had just come in, still wearing his straw hat.

'I explained to her that you had a few inquiries to make and that, as you didn't want to bother her in her distress, you preferred to question her daughter.'

'And the young lady?'

'We came on the bus, as you'd told me. I think she's a little nervous. She tried to find out what you wanted her for.'

'Bring her in.'

'There's an old gentleman asking to see you.'

'Afterwards . . . Let him wait . . . Who is it?'

'A shopkeeper from the Quai du Louvre . . . He insists on speaking to you personally.'

The air was as warm as on the previous day, with a slight haze like shining steam over the Seine, where strings of boats were sailing past.

Francine came in, dressed in a neat navy-blue suit over a white linen blouse. A spruce, demure young person with curly fair hair set off by a funny little red hat, and a high round bosom. She had obviously not had time, since the previous night, to buy herself mourning clothes.

'Sit down, Mademoiselle . . . And if you're too warm, you're welcome to take off your jacket.'

For there were beads of sweat on her upper lip.

'Your mother told me yesterday that you worked as a saleswoman at the Prisunic in the Rue Réaumur . . . If I remember rightly, it's just before the Boulevard Sébastopol, on the left?'

'Yes, Monsieur . . .'

Her lip was quivering, and Maigret sensed that there was something she was reluctant to disclose.

'Since the shop opens at nine o'clock, and since it's quite close to the Rue du Sentier, where your father was supposed to go every morning, I presume you used sometimes to travel together?'

'Sometimes . . .'

'You're sure of that?'

'It happened occasionally . . .'

'And did you leave him near his office?'

'Not far . . . At the corner of the street . . .'

'So that you never suspected?'

He was puffing gently at his pipe, looking benevolent as he watched the young face clouded by anxiety.

'I'm sure a young woman like yourself would never venture to lie to the police ... You realize how serious that would be, particularly now that we are trying our best to get hold of your father's murderer.'

'Yes, Monsieur.'

She had taken a handkerchief from her pocket and was dabbing her eyes, sniffing, ready to cry in real earnest.

'What pretty earrings you're wearing.'

'Oh, Monsieur ...'

'Yes, they're very pretty. May I have a look? It almost seems as if you've got a boyfriend already.'

'Oh, no, Monsieur.'

'They're made of real gold, and the two garnets are also real.'

'No, Monsieur ... Mother thought so too, but ...'

'But what?'

'... I told her they weren't ...'

'Because you bought these earrings yourself?'

'Yes, Monsieur.'

'Didn't you give your pay-packet to your parents?'

'Yes, Monsieur. But we'd agreed that I should keep my overtime pay for myself.'

'And you bought your handbag too?'

'Yes, Monsieur.'

'Tell me, my dear ...'

She looked up in surprise, and Maigret began to laugh.

'Have you finished?'

'What, Monsieur?'

'Trying to fool me.'

'I promise you ...'

'One moment, do you mind? ... Hello? Switchboard? Put me through to the Prisunic in the Rue Réaumur, will you?'

'Listen, Monsieur . . .'

He signed to her to be quiet and she burst into tears.

'Hello, Prisunic? . . . Will you put me through to the manager?
. . . Is that the manager speaking? . . . Police Judiciaire speaking.
I'd like some information, please, about one of your assistants,
Mademoiselle Francine Tremblet . . . Yes . . . What's that?
Three months ago? Thank you . . . I may call on you later in the
day . . .'

And turning to the girl:

'So there we are, Mademoiselle!'

'I was going to tell you . . .'

'When?'

'I was waiting to pluck up the courage . . .'

'How did it happen?'

'You won't tell mother? . . . It's because of her that I didn't
tell you right away . . . It's going to mean more weeping and
wailing . . . If you knew maman! . . . As I told you, I sometimes
travelled on the métro with father . . . To begin with he didn't
want me to go to work, and particularly not to take that job . . .
You understand? . . . But maman insisted that we weren't well
off, that she found it hard enough to make ends meet, that it was
an unexpected opportunity . . . It was she who introduced me to
the manager . . . Then one morning, about three months ago,
when I had left my father at the corner of the Rue du Sentier, I
realized that I'd left without any money . . . Mother had asked
me to buy various things in the neighbourhood . . . I ran after
papa. I saw that he didn't stop at Couvreur and Bellechasse's,
but went on through the crowd . . .

'I thought to myself that he was probably going to buy some
cigarettes or something . . . I was in a hurry . . . I went to the

shop ... Then as I had a free moment during the day I went along to papa's office ... And there they told me that he'd not been working there for a long time.'

'Did you speak to him that evening?'

'No ... Next day, I followed him ... He went towards the embankment and at one point he turned round and saw me. Then he said: "So much the better!"'

'Why *so much the better*?'

'Because he didn't like my working in a shop. He explained to me that he'd been wanting to get me out of it for a long time ... He told me that he'd changed his job, that he'd got a much better one, where he didn't have to be shut up indoors all day. That was when he took me into a shop and bought me these earrings ...

'"If your mother asks where you got them, tell her they're fake ..."'

'And since then?'

'I stopped working, but I didn't tell mother. Father made up my pay. From time to time we used to meet in town and go together to the pictures or the Jardin des Plantes.'

'You don't know what your father did all day?'

'No ... But I could see why he said nothing about it to mother. If he'd given her more money it would have made no difference ... There would always have been just as much mess at home ... It's hard to explain to someone who hasn't lived with us ... Maman means very well, but ...'

'Thank you, Mademoiselle.'

'Are you going to tell?'

'I don't know yet ... Did you ever meet your father with anybody?'

'No.'

'He never gave you any sort of address?'

'We always arranged to meet on the banks of the Seine, near the Pont-Neuf or the Pont des Arts . . .'

'One last question: when you met him on these occasions, was he always wearing the clothes he wore in the Rue des Dames?'

'Only once, a fortnight ago, he had on a grey suit that I'd never seen him in and that he never wore at home.'

'Thank you . . . Of course you've spoken to nobody about this?'

'Nobody.'

'No boyfriend in the offing?'

'No, honestly.'

He was in a good humour, quite groundlessly, since the problem was becoming more complicated instead of simpler. Perhaps he had been glad to find that his last night's hunch had not let him down? Perhaps, too, he was beginning to take a keen interest in Tremblet, the nobody who had spent years of his life concealing things and deceiving his lugubrious Juliette.

'Send in the old gentleman, Lucas . . .'

'He's Théodore Jussiaume, bird-fancier and vendor, Quai du Louvre. It's about the photograph.'

'It's about the photograph . . .'

'You recognized the victim?'

'I certainly did, Monsieur! One of my best customers.'

And so a new aspect of Maurice Tremblet was revealed. Once a week at least he spent quite a long while in Théodore Jussiaume's shop, which was loud with birdsong. He had a passion for canaries, and bought a great many of them.

'I've sold him at least three aviaries of the largest size.'

'Did you deliver them at his home?'

'No, Monsieur. He took them away himself in a taxi.'

22   'Did you not know his address?'

'Not even his name. One day he happened to mention that he was Monsieur Charles, and that was what we always called him, my wife and I and the assistants. He was a connoisseur, a real one. I often wondered why he didn't enter his canaries in competitions, for he had some real prizewinners among them.'

'Did he strike you as a wealthy man?'

'No, Monsieur . . . Comfortably off . . . He wasn't close-fisted, but he didn't waste his money.'

'In short, he was a good fellow?'

'An excellent fellow and a customer such as I seldom get.'

'He never brought anyone with him to your shop?'

'Never . . .'

'Thank you, Monsieur Jussiaume.'

But Monsieur Jussiaume was not ready to leave yet.

'There's one thing that puzzles me and worries me a bit . . . If the papers are telling the truth, there were no birds in the flat in the Rue des Dames . . . If all the canaries he had bought from me had been there it would surely have been mentioned, don't you see? Because there must have been about two hundred of them, and that's not an everyday thing . . .'

'In other words you're wondering if these birds . . .'

'Aren't somewhere or other without anyone to look after them, now that Monsieur Charles is dead . . .'

'Well, Monsieur Jussiaume, I promise you that if we find the canaries we'll let you know, so that you can attend to them if it's not too late.'

'Many thanks . . . It's my wife that's been worrying, chiefly.'

'A very good day to you, Monsieur Jussiaume.'

And, once the door was closed:

'What do you think of that, Lucas old man? Have you got the reports?'

23

The pathologist's report, to begin with. Dr Paul, in his conclusions, implied that Maurice Tremblet's death had really been accidental.

Forty lines of technical details of which the Superintendent understood nothing.

'Hello! Dr Paul? . . . Will you be kind enough to explain to me what you meant?'

That the bullet ought not to have pierced the victim's thorax, since it was not powerful, and if it had not accidentally struck a soft spot between two ribs it would never have reached the heart, but merely produced a superficial wound.

'He was unlucky, that's all!' concluded the doctor with the flowing beard. 'The shot had to be fired from a certain angle . . . and the man had to be in a certain position . . .'

'Do you think the murderer knew all this and aimed accordingly?'

'I think the murderer was an idiot . . . An idiot who's not a bad marksman, since he hit the man, but who would have been incapable of aiming so as to make sure of hitting the heart . . . To my mind, he's only got a hazy knowledge of firearms.'

And this report was confirmed by that of the ballistics expert Gastinne-Renette, according to whom the bullet – a twelve millimetre lead bullet – had been fired with an air-gun such as are used in fairgrounds.

One curious detail: the murderer had carefully filed down the tip of the bullet to make it sharper.

To a question from Maigret, the expert replied:

'Not at all! By this means he did not make it more lethal, quite the contrary! For a blunt bullet does more damage to the victim's flesh than a pointed one. The man who behaved in this way thought himself very clever, but knew nothing about firearms.'

'In short, an amateur?'

'An amateur who had misunderstood something that he'd read somewhere, maybe in some detective story.'

That was how far they had got by 11 a.m. on the day after Maurice Tremblet's death.

In the Rue des Dames, Juliette was wrestling with all her everyday problems, aggravated by those that result from the death of the head of the household, particularly when a murder is involved. To top everything, journalists assailed her from morning till night, and photographers lay in wait on the staircase.

'What did the Superintendent want to know?'

'Nothing, maman.'

'You're not telling me the truth . . . Nobody ever tells me the truth. Even your father used to lie to me, he lied to me for years . . .'

Her tears flowed; she sniffled as she spoke, as she did her housework, as she hustled her children, who had had to be dressed in black from head to foot for the funeral next day.

Somewhere, two hundred canaries were waiting to be given their daily food.

And Maigret said to Lucas with a sigh:

'All we can do is wait.'

Wait until the publication of the photographs produced some result, until somebody recognized Maurice Tremblet or Monsieur Charles!

During the past seven years, he must surely have been seen somewhere? If he changed his clothes away from home, if he bought birds and large aviaries he must have had somewhere to 25 go, a room, a flat or a house? He may have had a landlord, a concierge, a charwoman. Friends, maybe? Perhaps even a mistress?

It was all a bit crazy, and yet Maigret's feelings were somehow stirred by the case, although he would not have liked to admit it.

Nobodies don't get murdered.

And now he had begun to take an interest in this nobody, who had seemed so dim to begin with, this man whom he had never seen, whom he did not know from Adam and who had died in such an idiotic fashion, sitting on the edge of his bed beside dreary Juliette, struck by a bullet which ought never to have killed him.

A fairground rifle! . . . The sort of thing with which you shoot at clay pipes or at a little ball dancing on the tip of a jet of water.

And the murderer himself seemed to have been an insignificant fellow, patiently filing down the bullet in order to make it more lethal, and leaving behind him, in his bedroom at the *Hôtel Excelsior*, nothing but a dirty comb with broken teeth.

The murderer had a liver complaint. That was practically all that was known about him.

Lucas had gone off hunting again. A commonplace and unrewarding job; all the gunsmiths of Paris to be visited, then all the owners of shooting-booths, for the man might have bought his gun from one of them. Inspector Janvier, meanwhile, was questioning the trades-people of the Quai de la Mégisserie and the Quai du Louvre, and the bistros in the neighbourhood of the Pont-Neuf and the Pont des Arts, where Tremblet used to meet his daughter and where he might perhaps have had an occasional drink.

Finally Torrence, the big fellow, was questioning taxi drivers, since a fare carrying an outsize birdcage is hardly an everyday occurrence.

Maigret, meanwhile, was just sitting on the terrace of the *Brasserie Dauphine*, in the shade of the red and yellow striped awning, with a freshly drawn glass of beer in front of him. He was peacefully smoking his pipe, waiting till it was time to go home to lunch, and intermittently a brief frown clouded his forehead.

Something was worrying him, but he could not decide what it was. What had he been told, that morning or the night before, which had struck him, which must be important and which he had forgotten?

An insignificant little remark. And yet he had noted it, he was sure of that. He had even reflected that it might hold the key to the mystery.

He pondered. Could it have been while he was questioning the young girl with the high bosom and the red hat? . . . He ran over, in his mind, all that she had said to him . . . He pictured the scene in the Rue du Sentier, when she had run after her father, who was not going to his office.

The earrings? No . . . The father and daughter used to pay clandestine visits to the cinema . . . Francine, in short, was Tremblet's favourite. He must have felt proud to go out with her and buy her expensive presents secretly.

But that wasn't it . . . The little remark belonged elsewhere . . . Let's see . . . He had been standing in a slanting ray of sunlight, amid that fine golden dust that lingers so long in a room where the beds have just been made.

It was in the Rue des Dames . . . The door had been open on to the kitchen . . . It was Juliette speaking . . . What could she have said that for one moment had given him the impression that he was on the verge of understanding everything?

'Joseph! What do I owe you?'

'Four francs, Superintendent.'

All the way home he was trying to remember that little sentence. He went on thinking about it while he ate, elbows on the table, in his shirt-sleeves, and Madame Maigret, seeing him preoccupied, held her tongue.

She could not, however, resist murmuring as she set the fruit upon the table:

'Don't *you* think it's revolting that a man should . . .'

Of course! But Madame Maigret did not know Juliette. She did not know the flat in the Rue des Dames.

The little sentence was almost on the tip of his tongue. So his wife must have helped him involuntarily.

'Don't *you* think it's revolting . . .'

A tiny effort. It needed only a tiny effort, but the flash did not come, and he flung his napkin down upon the table, filled his pipe, poured himself a glass of calvados and went to lean on the window-sill until it was time to go back to the Quai des Orfèvres.

3   ON THE TRAIL OF AN ANGLER

At six o'clock the same evening, Maigret and Lucas got out of a taxi on the Quai de la Gare, beyond the Pont d'Austerlitz, accompanied by a little man with limp and shaggy hair who looked like a tramp.

And it was then, suddenly, that Maigret had an illumination, and the little sentence he had hunted for in vain recurred to his memory:

28   *'He had a horror of noise . . .'*

Tremblet, the nobody, the poor fellow who had been killed, in his shirt, rubbing his feet as he sat on the edge of the bed, Tremblet who lived in the Rue des Dames and who had five children each more mischievous than the other and a wife who spent her days moaning, Tremblet had a horror of noise.

There are people who have a horror of certain smells, others who shun heat or cold. Maigret remembered one divorce case in which the husband, after twenty-six or twenty-seven years of married life, pleaded for a separation on the grounds that he had never been able to get used to his wife's odour.

Tremblet had a horror of noise. And Tremblet, when circumstances that were still wrapped in mystery had enabled him to leave the offices of Messrs Couvreur and Bellechasse – in the noisy Rue du Sentier – had taken refuge on this quay, one of the most deserted in all Paris.

A broad embankment, beside which several rows of barges lay idle. An embankment that had a provincial flavour about it, with one-storey houses overlooking the Seine, a few blocks of flats, and bistros into which nobody seemed to go, and courtyards where, surprisingly, hens were scratching about on dunghills.

It was the ragged cripple, old Cerise, who had discovered the place; old Cerise who, as he declared grandly, resided under the nearest bridge, and who had been the first to turn up at Police Headquarters.

While he was waiting, three others had come, of different types but all of them down-and-outs, all belonging to that species of creature only to be found nowadays on the embankments of Paris.

'I'm the first, aren't I, Superintendent? I've been waiting half an hour . . . The others hadn't got here yet . . . So about the reward . . .'

'What reward?'

'Isn't there a reward?'

That would have been too unfair. The old fellow was indignant in anticipation.

'There's always a reward, even for a stray dog ... And I've come to tell you where that poor guy what got killed used to live ...'

'We'll see about giving you something if the information proves worth it.'

And there had been arguments and bargaining: a hundred francs, fifty francs, twenty francs – the lowest price. They had taken him along with them. Now they were standing in front of a small one-storey house, whitewashed, with closed shutters.

'Almost every morning I used to see him fishing, just here where the tug is ... That was how we got acquainted ... To begin with he wasn't very good at it, but I gave him some advice ... He used hemp-seed for bait. And thanks to me he used to catch some nice roach for frying ... At eleven o'clock sharp he would roll up his lines and tie up his rods and go home. That was how I found out where he lived.'

Maigret rang on the off-chance, and an old-fashioned bell echoed curiously in the empty house. Lucas tried out his master keys and eventually got the lock to play.

'I'll stay around,' said old Cerise, 'in case you may need me.'

There was something uncanny about this house that reeked of emptiness and where, nonetheless, sounds could be heard. It took a moment to realize that it was caused by the fluttering of birds.

For there were aviaries in both the ground floor rooms, and these rooms were almost eerie because apart from the cages they were almost totally unfurnished.

Maigret and Lucas went to and fro, and their voices echoed; they flung open doors, creating draughts that puffed out the curtains of the front room, the only one where there were any on the windows.

The wallpaper must have been there for countless years; it had faded to an indeterminate colour and showed the marks of all the furniture that had leaned against it, of all the tenants who had ever lived there.

The first thing that Maigret did, to Lucas's surprise, was to put fresh water into the birdcages and fill the trays with little shiny yellow grains.

'You see, old man? Here, at least, he was free from noise.'

There was an old-fashioned wicker armchair beside one of the windows, a table, two or three chairs that did not match, and on the shelves a collection of cloak-and-dagger stories and historical romances.

On the first floor a bed, a brass bedstead covered with a fine red satin eiderdown, shimmering in the sunlight, that would have rejoiced the heart of a prosperous farmer's wife.

A kitchen. Plates, a frying pan; and Maigret, sniffing it, recognized a strong smell of fish. Moreover there were still fishbones and scales in the dustbin, which had not been emptied for several days. In a closet there was a whole set of fishing rods, neatly arranged.

'Don't *you* think it's a funny idea?'

Evidently, Tremblet had his own notion of happiness. The peace of a house which no one entered but himself. Fishing on the banks of the Seine. He had a couple of folding stools, one of which was the latest model and probably very expensive. Birds in handsome cages. And books, heaps of books in gaudy covers which he could enjoy in peace.

The strangest thing was the contrast between some of these objects and the squalor of the setting. There was among other 31 things an English fishing rod which must have cost several thousand francs. In a drawer of the sole chest of drawers in the house there was a gold lighter bearing the initials M.T. and an expensive-looking cigarette case.

'Can you understand it, Chief?'

Yes, Maigret felt he could understand it. Particularly when he discovered some perfectly useless objects, such as an elaborate electric train.

'Don't you see, he'd been longing for these things for so many years . . .'

'Do you suppose he used to play with the electric train?'

'I shouldn't be surprised . . . Did you never treat yourself to something you'd dreamed of all through your childhood?'

Presumably, Tremblet came here in the morning, as another man might go to the office. He went fishing in front of his house. He returned to the Rue des Dames for lunch, perhaps after sometimes eating the fish he had caught. He looked after his birds. He read; he must have read for hours at a time, in his wicker armchair beside the window, without anyone to disturb him, without shouts and cries going on around him.

Some days he used to go to the cinema, occasionally with his daughter. And he had bought her a pair of gold earrings.

'Do you think he'd come into a legacy, or else stolen the money he spent like this?'

Maigret made no answer. He went on roaming through the house, in front of which old Cerise mounted guard.

'Go back to the Quai des Orfèvres. Circulate all the banks in Paris to find out whether Tremblet had an account there. Inquire from solicitors . . .'

It seemed unlikely, however. The man had too much prudence of the old peasant sort to deposit his money where it could be traced.

'Are you going to stay here?'

'I think I'll spend the night here ... Listen ... Bring me some sandwiches and a few bottles of beer ... Ring my wife and tell her I shall probably not be coming back ... See that the papers don't publish anything about this house.'

'Wouldn't you like me to come and keep you company or send an inspector?'

'It's not worth while.'

He was not armed. What was the point?

The hours that followed were not unlike those that Tremblet must have spent in the house. Maigret looked through a number of books in the strange library, and found that most of them had been read and re-read.

He spent a long time examining the fishing rods, for it had occurred to him that, for a man like Tremblet, they might prove an ideal hiding-place.

'Two thousand francs a month for seven years.'

It was quite a sum; not to mention all the further expenses that the man incurred. The hoard must be hidden somewhere.

At eight o'clock a taxi stopped at the door, while Maigret was searching the bird cages for a possible hiding-place.

It was Lucas, accompanied by a girl who looked in a very bad temper.

'As I couldn't ring you up, I didn't know what to do,' the sergeant said in some embarrassment. 'In the end I thought the best thing was to bring her along. She was his mistress.'

A tall dark girl with a pale face and hard features, who stared at the Superintendent suspiciously and remarked:

'I hope I'm not going to be accused of killing him?'

'Come in, come in,' Maigret said softly. 'You must know the house better than I do.'

'Me? I've never set foot in the filthy shack . . . I didn't even know of its existence until five minutes ago . . . Not to mention that the place doesn't smell nice . . .'

It was not her ear-drums that were sensitive; it was her nose. And she began by wiping the chair on which she was invited to sit down.

4   THE FOURTH LIFE OF MAURICE TREMBLET

Olga-Jeanne-Marie Poissonneau, twenty-nine years of age, born at Saint-Joris-sur-Isère, unemployed, residing at *Hôtel Beauséjour*, Rue Lepic, Paris XVIIIe.

And the tall, moon-faced girl hurriedly added: 'Please to observe, Superintendent, that I came forward of my own free will. As soon as I saw his picture in the papers, and in spite of the fact that it might spell trouble for me, I said to myself . . .'

'Did Tremblet visit you at your hotel?'

'Twice a week . . .'

'So that the proprietor and the staff must have seen him there?'

'Oh, they knew him very well. It's been going on for five years now . . .'

'And have they seen the photograph too?'

'What do you mean?'

She bit her lip, for she had finally caught on.

'Well, the landlord did ask me whether the photo wasn't of Monsieur Charles . . . I'd have come along all the same.'

'I'm sure you would. So you knew him under the name of Monsieur Charles?'

34 'I'd met him by chance outside a cinema in the Boulevard

Rochechouart ... I was a waitress at that time in a *prix fixe* restaurant in the Place Clichy. He followed me ... He told me he only came to Paris from time to time.'

'Twice a week ...'

'Yes ... The second or third time I met him he took me back to the hotel, and he went upstairs with me ... That's how it began ... It was he who insisted on my leaving my job ...'

Why had Tremblet picked her? Probably because Juliette was small and thin, a faded blonde, whereas this girl was tall, dark and soft-looking. The latter, particularly; presumably he had believed her moon-face was a sign of softness, perhaps of sentimentality.

'I soon realized that he was batty.'

'Batty?'

'A crank, anyhow ... He talked of nothing but taking me into the country ... That was his dream. When he came to see me we had to go into the public gardens and sit on a bench ... For months he nagged at me to spend a couple of days in the country with him, and he got his way at last ... I can tell you it wasn't much fun ...'

'Did he keep you?'

'He gave me just enough to live on ... I had to pretend I made my own dresses ... He'd have liked me to spend my days sewing and mending. Talk about freaks! ... Lots of times I've tried to get rid of him and told him a few home truths, but he clung on, he came back with presents and wrote me long letters ... What are you laughing at?'

'Nothing ...'

Poor Tremblet, seeking a change from a Juliette and landing himself with an Olga!

'So you must have spent a good part of your time together quarrelling?'

'Part of it, yes ...'

'And you never had the curiosity to follow him and find out where he lived?'

'He told me it was somewhere near Orléans, and I believed him . . . In any case, I was going to get rid of him.'

'You had another friend, obviously.'

'I had friends, sort of . . . But nothing serious.'

'Did you tell them about him?'

'You don't suppose I was proud of him! He looked like the verger of a poor parish.'

'You never saw him about with anybody else?'

'Never . . . I tell you his idea of fun was sitting with me on park benches . . . Is it true he was very rich?'

'Who told you that?'

'I read in the papers that he'd probably inherited a fortune . . . And here I am left without a penny! . . . *You'll admit it's just my luck . . .*'

She sounded just like Juliette.

'Do you think it's going to mean trouble for me?'

'No, no. Your evidence will be checked, that's all. Is that clear, Lucas?'

And inquiries confirmed her evidence, including the rows she had with her lover each time he visited her, for she had a vicious temper.

Maigret had spent that night and part of the next day searching through every nook and cranny of the house on the Quai de la Gare, but he had found nothing.

He had felt quite sorry to leave the house, where he had, as it were, become involved in the private life of his nobody, and he had had it discreetly watched day and night by detectives posted in the neighbourhood.

'We'll see what comes of it,' he had said to the Chief of the Police Judiciaire. 'It may take a long time, but I think it'll yield results in the end.'

Inquiries were made about Francine, who might have had a lover. Olga's movements were watched, and an eye was kept on the down-and-outs of the Quai de la Gare.

There was nothing to be got from banks or solicitors. Telegrams were sent to Tremblet's native Cantal, but it seemed certain that he had not come into any legacy.

The weather was still warm. Tremblet had been buried. His wife and children were preparing to leave for the provinces, for they could no longer afford to live in Paris.

The police now knew about Tremblet's life in the Rue des Dames, his life in the Quai de la Gare, his life with Olga . . . They knew him as a keen angler, a bird fancier and a reader of light fiction.

It was a waiter in a café who disclosed what might be described as the dead man's fourth existence. He appeared one morning at the Quai des Orfèvres and asked to speak to Maigret.

'I'm sorry not to have come sooner, but I was working at Les Sables d'Olonne for the summer season . . . I saw the photo in the paper, and I nearly wrote to you, then it went out of my head . . . I'm practically certain this was the guy who came for years to play billiards in the brasserie where I used to work, at the corner of the Boulevard Saint-Germain and the Rue de Seine.'

'He didn't play billiards all by himself?'

'Of course not . . . He used to come with a tall thin fellow, who had ginger hair and a moustache . . . The other, the man who was killed, called him Théodore, and they were on very intimate terms . . . They used to come in every day at the same

time, about four o'clock, and leave again just before six . . .
Théodore would have apéritifs, but the other guy never touched
alcohol.'

That is how one picks up people's tracks as they come and go
through a great city. Tremblet's had been discovered in the
bird-fancier's shop on the Quai du Louvre and in a shady hotel
in the Rue Lepic.

And now it became known that for years he had frequented a
quiet brasserie on the Boulevard Saint-Germain, in the company
of a tall fellow with red hair.

'Is it a long time since you saw them?'

'I left the place over a year ago.'

Torrence, Janvier, Lucas and other detectives then started
visiting all the cafés and brasseries of Paris where they have
billiard tables, and the trail of the two men was picked up again
in one not far from the Pont-Neuf, where they had played
billiards together for several months.

But nobody knew anything more about Théodore than the
fact that he was a hard drinker and had the habit of brushing up
his moustache with the back of his hand after every mouthful.

'He seemed to be in humble circumstances, and was poorly
dressed . . .'

It was invariably Tremblet who paid.

For weeks, the police searched everywhere for Théodore, and
Théodore remained untraceable, until one day Maigret happened
to think of calling on Messrs Couvreur et Bellechasse.

He was received by Monsieur Mauvre.

'Théodore? Why, we had an employee of that name a long
time ago . . . Let's see . . . It's over twelve years since he left the
firm . . . Of course he knew Monsieur Tremblet here . . . This
Théodore – I could discover his surname in our books – was a

38

messenger, and we had to get rid of him because he was always drunk and then permitted himself shocking liberties.'

His name was traced: Ballard. Théodore Ballard. But the lodging houses of Paris and the suburbs were searched in vain for any signs of a Théodore Ballard.

One fresh but inconclusive clue: five years previously a certain Théodore Ballard had worked for a few weeks at the Montmartre street fair, on a merry-go-round. He had broken his arm one night when he was drunk, and he had not been seen again.

This was obviously the man from the *Hôtel Excelsior*, the man with the air-gun.

How had he happened to renew acquaintance with the cashier of the firm where he had once been a messenger? In any case, the two men had formed the habit of meeting and playing billiards together.

Had Théodore discovered his friend's secret? Had he scented hidden treasure in the house on the Quai de la Gare? Or had there been a quarrel between the two friends?

'Keep up the watch on the embankment . . .'

And it was kept up. It had become a joke at Headquarters:

'What are you doing tonight?'

'Looking after the canaries . . .'

And yet in the long run it yielded a positive result, for one night a tall thin fellow with a reddish moustache, slouching along like a beggar, actually broke into the house.

Torrence pounced upon him, and the man begged for mercy.

If the victim had been shabby enough, so was the murderer. Théodore was a pitiful sight. He must have been several days without food, as he prowled about the streets and along the embankments. He probably suspected that the house was being watched, for he had waited a long time before venturing into it. In the end he had been unable to hold out any longer.

'Well, it can't be helped,' he sighed. 'It's better this way. I'm too hungry.'

At two in the morning he was still in Maigret's office, with beer and sandwiches before him, answering all the questions put to him.

'I'm no good, I know, but what you don't know is that he, Maurice, was a mean bastard ... He'd never told me, for instance, that he had a house on the quay ... He didn't trust me ... He was willing to play billiards with me but as far as anything else was concerned he kept himself to himself ... D'you understand? ... I sometimes borrowed small sums from him, but I had to prise them out of him ...'

'I may have gone too far ... I hadn't a penny. I was in arrears with my rent and then he told me it was the last time, that he was sick of playing the sucker and that he was bored with billiards anyway ...

'In short, he was giving me the sack like a servant.

'And that was when I followed him, and understood what sort of life he was leading, and I said to myself that there must be some money in the house ...'

'You killed him to begin with,' growled Maigret, sucking his pipe.

'That only proves that I'm not mercenary, because it was really anger that made me do it ... Otherwise I'd have gone first to the Quai de la Gare when I knew he wasn't there.'

That wretched house was searched by the most knowing experts ten times over and it was only a year later, when it had been sold and the whole affair had been forgotten, that the hoard was discovered.

It was neither in the walls nor under the floor-boards, but hidden in the depths of a disused closet on the first floor.

It was a fairly large parcel, done up in oil-cloth, and containing two million and several hundred thousand franc notes.

When Maigret heard the figure mentioned, he made a rapid calculation and understood; he jumped into a taxi, and got off in front of the Pavillon de Flore.

'Have you the list of all the winners in the National Lottery?'

'Not the complete list, for certain winners prefer to remain anonymous, and they're entitled to by law. For instance, seven years ago . . .'

It was Tremblet, Tremblet who had won three million and carried them off, in notes, under his arm, Tremblet who had never breathed a word of it to anyone, Tremblet who had a horror of noise and who, henceforward, had treated himself to the modest delights he had so much longed for.

'Nobodies don't get murdered . . .'

And yet it had really been a nobody who had died, clad only in his shirt, sitting on the edge of his bed and rubbing his feet before slipping between the sheets.

15 August 1946

The Man in the Street

The four men were packed close together in the taxi. Paris was in the grip of frost. At half-past seven in the morning, the city looked leaden, and the wind drove powdery rime across the ground.

The thinnest of the four men, on a folding seat, had a cigarette stuck to his lower lip and handcuffs on his wrists. The biggest of them, a heavy-jawed man in a thick overcoat and a bowler hat, was smoking a pipe and watching the railings of the Bois de Boulogne race past.

'Would you like me to put up a lovely fight?' the hand-cuffed man proposed amiably. 'With writhing, cursing, foaming at the mouth, the lot?'

And Maigret growled, as he took the cigarette from the man's lips and opened the car door, since they had now reached the Porte de Bagatelle:

'Don't you try and be too clever!'

The avenues in the Bois were deserted, as white as limestone and as hard. A dozen people were kicking their heels at the corner of a woodland ride, and a photographer attempted to take a picture of the group as they approached. But Louis the Kid, as he had been instructed, held his arms in front of his face.

Maigret looked slowly round like a sulky bear, noticing everything, the new blocks of flats in the Boulevard Richard-Wallace, with their shuttered windows, a few workmen on bicycles coming in from Puteaux, a tram with its lights on, a couple of concierges approaching, their hands purple with cold.

42   'All set?' he asked.

The day before, he had had the following paragraph inserted in the newspapers:

THE CRIME AT BAGATELLE

This time the police have not been slow in clearing up a case that appeared to present insuperable difficulties. As has already been stated, on Monday morning a park-keeper in the Bois de Boulogne discovered on one of the walks, some hundred metres from the Porte de Bagatelle, a body which was identified on the spot as that of Ernest Borms, a well-known Viennese doctor, who had been living in Neuilly for some years.

Borms was in evening dress. He must have been attacked during the Sunday night as he was returning to his flat in the Boulevard Richard-Wallace.

He was shot point-blank through the heart with a small calibre revolver.

Borms was a youngish man, handsome and very well-dressed, who moved in fashionable society.

Scarcely forty-eight hours after this murder, the Criminal Investigation Department have made an arrest. Tomorrow morning, between seven and eight, a reconstitution of the crime will take place on the spot.

Later on, at Police Headquarters, this case was to be cited as particularly characteristic of Maigret's method; but when it was spoken of in his presence, he had a peculiar habit of averting his head with a growl.

Well! Everything was ready. Almost no loiterers, as he had foreseen. It was not without good reason that he had chosen such an early hour. In fact, among the ten or fifteen people who were kicking their heels were a number of detectives wearing their most innocent air; one of them, Torrence, who adored dressing up, had disguised himself as a milkman, which caused Maigret to shrug his shoulders.

Provided Louis the Kid didn't overdo things! . . . He was an old acquaintance of the police and had been arrested the day before for picking pockets in the métro . . .

'You can lend us a hand tomorrow morning and we'll see to it that you get off lightly this time . . .'

He had been taken out of the cells.

'Let's go!' growled Maigret. 'When you heard footsteps you were hiding in this corner, weren't you?'

'Just as you say, Superintendent . . . I was starving, you see . . . Absolutely broke! . . . So I said to myself that a big shot in a dinner jacket on his way home must have plenty of dough on him . . . "Your money or your life," I breathe in his ear . . . And I give you my word it wasn't my fault if the gun went off. I think it was the cold that made my finger press the trigger . . .'

11 a.m. Maigret was prowling about his room in the Quai des Orfèvres, smoking his pipe and fiddling endlessly with the telephone.

'Hello! Is that you, Chief? It's Lucas . . . I followed the old boy who seemed to be interested in the reconstruction . . . Nothing doing there . . . He's a crank who goes for a walk in the Bois every morning . . .'

'All right! You can come back.'

11.15 a.m. 'Hello, Chief? This is Torrence. I shadowed the young man you tipped me the wink about . . . He's a salesman in a Champs-Elysées shop, who's hoping to become a private inquiry agent . . . Shall I come back?'

Not until 11.55 was there a call from Janvier.

'I'm working fast, Chief . . . I'm afraid the bird may get away . . . I'm watching him in the little mirror set in the door of the phone box . . . I'm at the *Nain Jaune* bar in the Boulevard Roche-chouart . . . Yes . . . He spotted me . . . He's not got a clear conscience . . . As we crossed the Seine he threw something into the river. He's tried to lose me about ten times . . . Shall I wait for you here?'

And thus began a chase which was to go on for five days and five nights, through a city that was unaware of it, among hurrying pedestrians, from bar to bar, from bistro to bistro, Maigret and his detectives taking it in turns to pursue a solitary man and becoming, in the end, as exhausted as their quarry.

Maigret alighted from his taxi in front of the *Nain Jaune*, at apéritif time, and found Janvier leaning against the counter. He made no effort to assume an innocent air; quite the reverse!

'Which is he?'

With a jerk of his chin the detective indicated a man sitting at a small table in a corner. The man was watching them with pale blue-grey eyes that gave his face a foreign look. A Scandinavian or a Slav? Probably the latter. He wore a grey overcoat, a well-cut suit, a soft felt hat.

'What'll you drink, Chief? A hot *picon*?'

'Hot *picon* be it . . . What's he drinking?'

'A brandy . . . the fifth since this morning . . . You mustn't mind if my speech is a bit slurred, but I've had to follow him into every bistro . . . He's tough, you know. Look at him . . . he's been like that all morning. He wouldn't drop his eyes for the world.'

It was quite true. And it was odd. One could not call it arrogance or defiance. The man was simply looking at them. If he was feeling anxious, he did not show it. His face expressed sadness, rather; but a calm, thoughtful sadness.

'At Bagatelle, when he noticed that you were watching him, he immediately moved away and I followed suit. He turned round before he'd gone a hundred metres. Then instead of leaving the 45

Bois as he had apparently meant to, he strode off down the first walk he came to. He turned round again. He recognized me. He sat down on a bench, in spite of the cold, and I stopped . . . On several occasions I had the feeling that he wanted to speak to me, but he always ended by shrugging his shoulders and moving off again . . .

'At the Porte Dauphine I nearly lost him, for he jumped into a taxi, and it was only by sheer luck that I found another almost immediately. He got out in the Place de l'Opéra and rushed into the métro. One behind the other, we changed lines five times, and he began to understand that he wouldn't get rid of me that way . . .

'We came up above ground again. We were in the Place Clichy. Since then we've been going from bar to bar . . . I was waiting for a convenient place with a telephone booth from which I could keep an eye on him. When he saw me telephoning he gave a sort of bitter little laugh . . . And afterwards one would have sworn he was expecting you . . .'

'Ring them up at the "office" . . . Tell Lucas and Torrence to be ready to join me at short notice . . . And a photographer from the Records Department with a very small camera . . .'

'Waiter!' the stranger called out. 'How much?'

'Three francs fifty.'

'I'm willing to bet he's a Pole,' Maigret whispered to Janvier. 'Let's go . . .'

They did not get far. In the Place Blanche they followed the man into a small restaurant and sat down at the table next to his. It was an Italian restaurant, and they ate pasta.

At three o'clock Lucas came to take over from Janvier, who was sitting with Maigret in a brasserie opposite the Gare du Nord.

'The photographer?' Maigret inquired.

'He's waiting to catch the man when he comes out.'

46   And when the Pole left the place, after reading the newspapers,

a detective stepped up briskly towards him. When he was less than a yard away the click of a camera was heard. The man swiftly covered his face with his hand, but it was too late, and then, showing that he had understood, he cast a reproachful glance at the Superintendent.

'It's clear, my friend,' Maigret soliloquized, 'that you've some good reasons for not taking us to your home. But however much patience you have, mine's at least equal to yours . . .'

By evening a few snowflakes were drifting in the streets, while the stranger walked about, his hands in his pockets, waiting for bed-time.

'Shall I relieve you for the night, Chief?' Lucas proposed.

'No! I'd rather you saw to the photograph. Consult the files first of all. Then ask around in foreigners' circles. He's no recent arrival; somebody must know him.'

'Suppose we published his picture in the papers?'

Maigret gave his subordinate a contemptuous glance. So Lucas, who had worked with him for so many years, didn't understand? Had the police got a single piece of evidence? Not one! A man had been killed at night in the Bois de Boulogne; no weapon had been found, no fingerprints; Dr Borms lived alone, and his one servant did not know where he had been the night before.

'Do as I tell you. Off with you . . .'

Finally, at midnight, the man brought himself to enter a hotel. Maigret followed. It was a second-rate, indeed a third-rate hotel.

'I want a room . . .'

'Will you fill in the form?'

He did so, hesitantly, his fingers numb with cold. He looked Maigret up and down, as if to say:

'If you think this worries me! . . . I can write whatever I fancy.' 47

And he put down a name at random: Nicolas Slaatkovitch, arrived in Paris the previous day.

It was obviously false. Maigret rang the Police Judiciaire. The records of lodging houses and registers of foreigners were searched; inquiries were made to frontier police. There was no sign of any Nicolas Slaatkovitch.

'A room for you too?' asked the proprietor somewhat resentfully, for he had recognized a policeman.

'No, thanks. I shall spend the night on the stairs.'

It seemed safer. He sat down on a step in front of the door of room number seven. Twice the door opened. The man peered into the darkness, caught sight of Maigret's figure and eventually went back to bed. In the morning his beard had grown and his cheeks were rough. He had not been able to change his shirt. He had not even a comb with him, and his hair was dishevelled.

Lucas appeared.

'Shall I take over, Chief?'

But Maigret could not bring himself to leave the stranger. He watched him pay for his room. He saw him turn pale, and he guessed.

A little later, in fact, in a bar where, practically side by side, they drank *café crème* and ate croissants, the man openly counted his store of wealth. One hundred-franc note, two twenty-franc pieces and one piece of ten, plus some small change. His lips twisted in a bitter grin.

Well, he wouldn't get far with that. When he came to the Bois de Boulogne he must just have left home, for he had freshly shaven cheeks and clothes without a speck of dust or a crease. He had probably expected to be back shortly afterwards; he hadn't even looked to see what money he had in his pockets.

What he had thrown into the Seine, Maigret guessed, must have been identity papers and possibly visiting cards.

At all costs, he wanted to prevent anyone finding out where he lived.

And he set off again on the long, weary ramble of the homeless, lingering in front of shops and stalls, entering bars from time to time for somewhere to sit and take refuge from the cold, reading newspapers in brasseries.

A hundred and fifty francs! No restaurant for him at midday; he had to content himself with hard-boiled eggs, which he ate standing up at a bar counter, washed down with a glass of beer, while Maigret devoured sandwiches.

The man hesitated for a long time in front of a cinema, wondering whether to go in. He fingered the coins in his pocket. Better try and last out . . . He went on walking, walking . . .

In fact, one detail struck Maigret: this exhausting ramble always followed the same course, through the same districts: between the Trinité and Place Clichy, between Place Clichy and Barbès by way of the Rue Caulaincourt, then from Barbès to the Gare du Nord and the Rue La Fayette . . .

Was the man afraid of being recognized elsewhere? Surely, he had chosen the districts farthest from his home or his hotel, those which he did not habitually visit . . .

Did he, like so many foreigners, frequent the Montparnasse district? The neighbourhood of the Panthéon?

To judge by his clothes, he was moderately well-off; they were comfortable, quiet and well-cut. A professional man, no doubt. Maigret noticed that he wore a wedding ring.

Maigret had had to resign himself to handing over his place to Torrence. He had hurried home. Madame Maigret was disappointed, because her sister had come on a visit from Orléans and

49

she had prepared a special dinner, and now her husband, after shaving and changing, was off again, announcing that he didn't know when he would be back.

He made straight for the Quai des Orfèvres.

'Anything for me from Lucas?'

Yes. There was a message from the inspector. He had passed round the photograph in a number of Polish and Russian circles. Nobody knew the man. Nor was there anything to be learnt from the various political groups. As a last resort he had had a great many copies of the photograph printed; in every part of Paris policemen went from door to door, inquiring from concierges, and showing the document to the landlords of bars and the waiters in cafés.

'Hello! Superintendent Maigret? I'm an usherette at the news-cinema in the Boulevard de Strasbourg . . . There's a gentleman here, Monsieur Torrence . . . He told me to call you to say that he's here, but daren't leave the hall . . .'

It was cunning of the man; he had reckoned that this was the warmest place to spend a number of hours at little expense . . . Two francs entry . . . and you could stay on for several performances!

A curious intimacy had sprung up between the hunter and the hunted, between the man with the unshaven chin and rumpled clothes and Maigret, who kept stubbornly on his trail. There was even one comical detail; they had both caught colds. Their noses were red. Almost rhythmically, they pulled out their handkerchiefs, and once the man gave an involuntary smile on seeing Maigret give a whole series of sneezes.

After sitting through five consecutive programmes at the news-cinema, they moved on to a squalid hotel in the Boulevard de la Chapelle. The man signed the same name on the register.

And Maigret, once again, settled down on the staircase. But since this was a hotel frequented by prostitutes, he was disturbed every ten minutes by couples who stared at him with curiosity, and the women felt uneasy.

Would the man make up his mind to go home once his money was spent or when he was at the end of his tether? In a brasserie where he stayed for some length of time and took off his grey overcoat, Maigret seized hold of this without hesitation and examined the inside of the collar. It bore the label of the 'Old England' shop in the Boulevard des Italiens. It was a ready-made garment, and the shop must have sold dozens like it. Maigret noticed one significant piece of evidence: it was a year old. So the stranger must have been in Paris for a year at least. And during that year he must have stayed somewhere . . .

Maigret had begun drinking toddies to get rid of his cold. The stranger was becoming close-fisted; he drank only coffee, not even laced with spirits, and ate hard-boiled eggs and croissants.

The news from the 'office' was still the same: nothing to report! Nobody had recognized the photograph of the Pole, and no missing person had been reported.

Nor was there any further information about the dead man. He had earned a good income, took no interest in politics, led a busy social life, and since he specialized in nervous diseases his patients were chiefly women.

Maigret had never yet had occasion to study the question of how long it takes for a well-bred, well-dressed, well-groomed man to lose his gloss once he is turned out into the streets.

He knew, now, that it took four days. The beard, for one thing. The first morning the man looked like a lawyer, a doctor, 51 an architect or an industrialist, and one could imagine him living in a comfortable flat. A four-day beard had transformed him so much that if his picture had been published in connection with the Bois de Boulogne affair people would have declared: 'He's obviously a murderer!'

The cold air and the lack of sleep had reddened his eyelids, and there was a hectic flush on his cheekbones. His shoes were unpolished and shapeless, his overcoat looked shabby and his trousers bagged at the knees.

Even his gait . . . He no longer walked in the same way . . . He slunk along by the wall . . . He lowered his eyes when people looked at him as they passed . . . One further point: he averted his head when he went past a restaurant where customers were sitting in front of well-filled plates . . .

'Your last twenty francs, poor fellow!' Maigret reckoned. 'And what next?'

Lucas, Torrence and Janvier relieved him from time to time, but he gave up his post to them as seldom as possible. He would burst into his chief's office at Police Headquarters.

'You ought to take a rest, Maigret . . .'

Peevish and prickly, Maigret seemed torn by conflicting feelings. 'Is it or isn't it my job to catch the murderer?'

'Obviously . . .'

'Then I'm off!' he sighed with a touch of resentment in his voice. 'I wonder where we shall go to bed tonight?'

Only twenty francs left, not even that! When he rejoined Torrence, the latter informed him that the man had eaten three hard-boiled eggs and drunk two coffees, laced with brandy, in a bar at the corner of the Rue Montmartre.

'Eight francs fifty . . . He's got eleven fifty left . . .'

He admired the man. Far from trying to conceal himself he

walked level with him, sometimes right beside him, and had to control an impulse to speak to him.

'Come on, old chap! Don't you think it's time for a meal? . . . Somewhere or other there's a warm home waiting for you, a bed, slippers, a razor . . . eh? And a good dinner . . .'

The man, however, went on prowling aimlessly under the arc lamps of the Halles, among the heaps of cabbages and carrots, stepping aside when he heard the whistle of a train, avoiding market gardeners' trucks.

'You won't be able to afford a room!'

The Meteorological Office that evening registered eight degrees below zero. The man treated himself to hot sausages from an open-air stall. He would reek of garlic and burnt fat all night!

At one point he tried to slip into a shed and lie down in one corner. A policeman, to whom Maigret had not had time to give instructions, sent him packing. Now he was limping. The Quais. The Pont des Arts – provided he didn't take it into his head to throw himself into the Seine! Maigret felt he would not have the courage to jump in after him into the black water, where ice was beginning to drift.

He walked along the tow-path. Some tramps were grumbling; under the bridges, the best places were already taken.

In a little street near the Place Maubert, through the windows of a strange tavern, old men could be seen asleep, their heads on the table. For twenty sous, a glass of red wine included! The man looked at Maigret through the darkness. Then, with a fatalistic shrug, he pushed open the door. Before it had closed, Maigret caught a nauseating whiff; he decided to remain outside. Summoning a constable on the beat, he posted him as sentry on the pavement while he went off to ring Lucas, who was on duty that night.

'We've been hunting for you for the past hour, Chief! We've found out who the man is, thanks to a concierge . . . His name's Stephan Strevzki, thirty-four years old, born in Warsaw; he's been living in France for the past three years . . . He's married to a fine-looking Hungarian girl called Dora . . . They rent a twelve thousand franc flat in Passy, in the Rue de la Pompe . . . Nothing to do with politics . . . The concierge has never seen the murdered man . . . Stephan went out on Monday morning earlier than usual . . . She was surprised not to see him come back, but she didn't worry because . . .'

'What's the time now?'

'Half-past three . . . I'm alone at Headquarters . . . I've had some beer brought up, but it's very cold!'

'Listen, Lucas . . . You're to . . . Yes, I know! Too late for the morning ones, but in the evening ones . . . Understood?'

That morning an indefinable odour of poverty seemed to cling to the man's very clothes. His eyes were more sunken. The glance he threw at Maigret, in the pale dawn, was one of pathetic reproachfulness.

Had he not been brought, gradually but yet at a dizzying speed, to the lowest rung of the ladder? He pulled up the collar of his overcoat. He did not leave the district. He dived into a bistro which had just opened, and there drank four brandies in quick succession, as though to drive away the appalling after-taste that the night had left in his throat and his breast.

Now there was nothing left for him but to keep on walking along streets slippery with frost. He must be aching in every limb; he was limping with the left leg. From time to time he halted and looked around despairingly.

Since he no longer went into cafés where there was a telephone,

Maigret could not be relieved. Back to the Quais! And there the man almost automatically fingered the secondhand books, turning their pages, occasionally checking the authenticity of a print or an engraving. An icy wind swept the Seine. As the barges moved forward, the water made a clinking sound due to the clashing of tiny fragments of ice.

From afar off, Maigret could see the Police Judiciaire building and the window of his office. His sister-in-law must have gone back to Orléans. If only Lucas . . .

He did not know, as yet, that this appalling case was going to become a classic, and that generations of detectives would relate it in every detail to their juniors. Absurdly, what disturbed him most was a trivial detail; the man had a spot on his forehead, which, looked at closely, would probably prove to be a boil, and which was turning from red to purple.

If only Lucas . . .

At midday, the man, who unquestionably knew his Paris well, made his way towards the paupers' soup kitchen at the far end of the Boulevard Saint-Germain. He joined the queue of down-and-outs. An old man spoke to him, but he pretended not to understand. Then another, whose face was pitted with smallpox, addressed him in Russian.

Maigret crossed over to the pavement on the other side of the street, and after a moment's hesitation yielded to the irresistible urge to enter a bistro and eat sandwiches; he turned away so that the man, if he looked through the window, should not see him eating.

The poor fellows moved on slowly, and were let in four or five at a time to the hall where they were given bowls of hot soup. The queue grew longer. From time to time someone would push at the back, and the others protested.

1 p.m. The newsboy came running from the far end of the street, leaning forward eagerly.

'Paper! Paper! *L'Intransigeant . . . L'Intran . . .*'

He, too, was trying to forestall his rivals. He could spot likely purchasers from afar. He paid no attention to the line of paupers.

'Paper . . .'

Humbly the man raised his hand, saying 'Pssstt!'

People in the queue looked at him. So he still had a few sous for a paper?

Maigret, too, hailed the newsboy, unfolded the paper, and found to his relief, on the front page, what he was looking for: the photograph of a young woman, smiling and beautiful.

MISSING WOMAN

A young Polish woman, Mme Dora Strevzki, is said to have disappeared four days ago from her home in Passy, 17 Rue de la Pompe. A disturbing factor in the case is that the husband of the missing woman, M. Stephan Strevzki, also disappeared from his home the day before, Monday, and the concierge, who informed the police, stated . . .

The man, borne forward by the moving queue, had only five or six paces more to go to get his bowl of steaming soup. At that very moment he stepped out of line, crossed the street, nearly got knocked over by a bus, but reached the pavement just as Maigret stood in front of him.

'I'm all yours,' he declared quite simply. 'Take me off . . . I'll answer all your questions.'

Everyone was waiting in the passage at Police Headquarters, Lucas, Janvier, Torrence, and others who had not been working on the case but knew about it. As they passed, Lucas gave Maigret a sign that meant: 'It's all right!'

A door opened and then shut. Beer and sandwiches were on the table.

'Have something to eat first . . .'

Embarrassed, the man could scarcely swallow. Then at last he said:

'Since she's gone away and is safe somewhere . . .'

Maigret felt impelled to turn and poke the stove.

'When I read about the murder in the paper . . . I'd suspected for quite some time that Dora was having an affair with that man . . . I knew she was not his only mistress . . . I knew Dora with her impulsive character . . . D'you understand? If he had tried to get rid of her, I knew she was capable of . . . And she had a pearl-handled revolver, she always carried it in her bag . . . When the papers announced the capture of the murderer and the reconstruction of the crime, I wanted to watch . . .'

Maigret would have liked to say, like an English policeman: 'I warn you that anything you say may be taken down and used in evidence . . .'

The man had kept on his hat and overcoat.

'Now that she's safe . . . For I suppose . . .' He cast an anxious look around, as a sudden suspicion crossed his mind. 'She must have understood, when she saw that I'd not come back . . . I knew it would end like that, I knew Borms was not the man for her and that she'd come back to me . . . She went out alone on Sunday evening, as she had taken to doing recently . . . She must have killed him when . . .'

Maigret blew his nose; he took a long time blowing it. A ray of sunlight, that bleak winter sunlight that goes with icy weather, came in through the window. The boil was gleaming on the man's forehead; Maigret could only think of him as 'the man'.

'Yes, your wife killed him . . . When she realized that he was   57 not serious about her ... And *you* realized that she had killed him ... And you didn't want ...'

He suddenly went up close to the Pole.

'I'm sorry, old fellow,' he muttered as though he was speaking to an old friend, 'I had to get at the truth, hadn't I? It was my duty to ...'

He opened the door.

'Bring in Madame Dora Strevzki ... Lucas, you carry on, I'm going to ...'

And nobody saw him again at Headquarters for two days. The director rang him up at home.

'Look here, Maigret ... You know that she's confessed everything and that ... By the way, how's your cold? I gather ...'

'It's nothing at all. It's all right ... In twenty-four hours ... And how is he?'

'What? ... Who? ...'

'The man!'

'Ah, I follow ... He's engaged the best lawyer in Paris ... He hopes ... You know, crimes of passion ...'

Maigret went back to bed and doped himself with aspirin and hot toddies. Later on, when anyone asked him about the investigation, he would growl discouragingly:

'What investigation?'

And the man came to see him once or twice a week to keep him informed about the lawyer's hopes.

The result was not outright acquittal: a year with remission of sentence.

And it was from this man that Maigret learnt to play chess.

1939

READ MORE IN PENGUIN